WHOSE EYE AM I ?

by YLLA
Story by Crosby Bonsall

Planned by Charles Rado

Designed by Luc Bouchage

Harper & Row, Publishers New York, Evanston, and London

1817

WHOSE EYE AM I ? • Printed in Switzerland for Harper & Row, Publishers,
Incorporated, 1968. All rights reserved. For information address
Harper & Row, Publishers, Incorporated, 49 East 33rd Street, New York, N.Y. 10016.
Library of Congress Catalog Card Number: 68-24336.

One eye.

One eye in a hole in a fence on a farm.

One boy sees one eye

in a hole in a fence on a farm.

Whose eye?

"Whose eye am I?" asks the voice of the eye

in the hole in the fence on the farm.

The boy hears it. The wind hears it

and carries the question across the farm.

Each creature hears it.

"Whose eye am I?"

The boy runs off to find out.

"If it were my eye, I wouldn't tell you, so run along
and stare at somebody else," snaps the rooster.
"I must practice crowing."

The turkeys gobble their gossip
softly to themselves.
One turkey objects to the boy.
"Gape, gape," she grumbles,
"gawp, gawp. Eyes like saucers
and a mouth like a canyon.
That's an idle boy for you!"
The boy runs on.

Six eyes in a field on a farm.

"Is it your eye?" the boy asks.

One horse looks skeptical. "Is this a joke?

If it is, my cousin over there will laugh at anything."

His cousin whickers and nickers and neighs.

"I'd love to help you," he chortles and snortles,

"but I'm" [gasp and whicker]

"simply" [snortle and snuffle] "crying too hard.

I" [wheeze and nicker] "always cry"

[gurgle and choke] "when I laugh." [Sniffle.]

"Some joke," says his sour friend.

The boy sees four more eyes.

"I have two eyes," says the colt,

"but my left one seems to have something in it.

If you're giving one away, I'll take it."

"I'm looking to *find* one," the boy says.

The beautiful white creature in the next pasture

snorts and rears. Is it that proud eye, the boy wonders.

But he runs on to look some more.

The cow gazes gently at him. "Why honey," she drawls,
"if you're looking for big brown melting eyes, I'm it."
The boy isn't sure and goes to look at the bull's eye.

The bull is having trouble with his tongue.
"Thtop thtaring," he cries,
"my eyeth are my own bithneth."
His sister Daisy scratches her head.
"But he must find an eye," she explains.
"An eye in a hole in a fence," says the boy.
"Daithy," says the bull,
"he thertainly talkth thilly."

The boy watches a calf for a long time. But the summer sun
is a sun for sleeping, and the calf won't open his eyes.
"Foolish," says the small donkey, "why don't you look at me?
I'm awake. Won't my eye do?"
One eye in a hole in a fence.
The boy runs into the woods to think.

"Mercy me," says a raccoon, "you might frighten
  a body half out of her wits staring like that."
"I'm sorry," the boy says. "I'm looking for an eye."
"Well, you're bound to find it if you keep on like that.
  Course, frightening folks isn't nice.
  Didn't your mama ever teach you not to stare?
  Try squinting a little."
The boy nods and squints at a squirrel.
One eye in a hole in the fence.

"Is it one of us? Is it one of us?" tease the doves.

"'Tain't me," croaks the frog. The boy runs into the barn.

"Wake a fellow up in the middle of the day just to look at
his eyes?" squawks the owl. "You've lost your senses, boy."

Outside, the boy cries to the dogs, "I must find that eye."

"Is this one of those treasure hunts?" the collie wants to know.

"Because if it is, I simply cannot be bothered.

On the other hand, if there are any little prizes such as a soupbone

or a small shrimp, I might be persuaded to play."

"Eyes," groans the Saint Bernard.

"My tooth is killing me, and you speak of eyes."

"Sorry," the boy says and leaves quietly.

The pigs are not happy
to see the boy either.
"It's lunchtime,"
complains the mother pig,
"and you're in the way,
and I've no room
for an extra guest.
Run along now.
You won't find the eye here."
Six hungry little pigs
don't say a word.
Their mouths are full.

In the next field the goat whispers to the kid.

"The pig is right. Boys are a terrible nuisance.

Don't pay any attention to him, and maybe he'll go away."

"You're too hard on the boy," says a bearded old goat.

"He thinks the answer to his problem will be in an eye.

I am positive the answer lies in a beard."

"*I* am positive
the answer lies in a tongue,"
thinks a little lamb
who has been listening.
There is no time to argue;
he follows his cousins
into the barn.
Every eye is closed.

Two kids
are playing tag
in the field.
"We know whose eye it is,
we know whose eye it is,"
they shout.
"But we'll never tell.

It's someone round
and someone soft
and someone shy
and someone sweet,
and you're cold, cold, cold
if you stay
around here."

The boy looks down at his feet and sees the puppy.

Someone round and someone soft.

The puppy looks boldly at the boy. He's not shy.

"Ssssst," hisses the cat. "You are really a very stupid boy.

I doubt if you can look me in the eye

and tell me who I am."

The boy looks him in the eye. "You're a cat," he says,

'but you're not sweet." And he keeps looking.

"I've looked and looked," the boy cries.

"I've run round and round this farm.

The cat is right. I'm stupid!"

The rabbit looks up shyly from between his paws.

"Don't mind the cat," he says softly.

"Cats are very self-centered.

Just keep on looking. That's the best way."

And the rabbit hops behind a fence.

"Hey!" cries the boy.

"That's the eye!"

The eye in the hole in the fence.

"Whose eye am I?" asks the rabbit.

Small and soft and shy.

"The rabbit! The rabbit!" cries the boy.

"I knew it all the time!"

"I'm sure you did," said the rabbit sweetly.

DATE DUE

5/18/71			
9-21-72			
4-24-73			
12-13-73			
2-5-74			
2-19-74			
11-22-74			
10-9-79			
3-26-77			
10-6-80			
10-28-80			
11/7/80			
12-21-83			
3-4-87			